This book belongs to

....

First published in 2013 by Miles Kelly Publishing Ltd
Harding's Barn, Bardfield End Green, Thaxted, Essex, CM6 3PX, UK

Copyright © Miles Kelly Publishing Ltd 2013

2 4 6 8 10 9 7 5 3 1

Publishing Director Belinda Gallagher
Creative Director Jo Cowan
Editorial Director Rosie McGuire
Senior Designer Joe Jones
Production Manager Elizabeth Collins
Reprographics Stephan Davis, Jennifer Hunt, Thom Allaway

All rights reserved. No part of this publication may be reproduced, stored in a retrieval system, or transmitted by any means, electronic, mechanical, photocopying, recording or otherwise, without the prior permission of the copyright holder.

ISBN 978-1-78209-288-9

Printed in China

British Library Cataloguing-in-Publication Data
A catalogue record for this book is available from the British Library

ACKNOWLEDGEMENTS

The publishers would like to thank the following artists
who have contributed to this book:

Cover and insides (main): Karen Sapp at The Bright Agency
Decorative banners (cover and throughout): asmjp from Shutterstock.com

Made with paper from a sustainable forest

www.mileskelly.net   info@mileskelly.net

www.factsforprojects.com

Little Red Riding Hood

Miles
Kelly

There was once a little girl who lived in the middle of a forest with her mother and father. The little girl always wore a red cloak

Little Red Riding Hood

with a hood, and, because of
this, everyone always called
her Little Red Riding Hood.

One day Little Red Riding
Hood decided to visit her
granny, who lived in another
part of the forest. She took a
basket with a cake baked by

her mother, and set off.

Now the last thing her mother said to Little Red Riding Hood was, "Don't leave the path, and don't talk to any strangers." But I am afraid Little Red Riding Hood was not really

listening, so when she saw
some flowers growing under
a tree she left
the path and
began to
pick them.
She thought
that a nice

bunch of bluebells would make a lovely present to give to her granny.

Slowly she wandered further away from the path, deeper into the trees. Suddenly, she realized that she was not alone. There in front of her

Little Red Riding Hood

stood a great big wolf.

Little Red Riding Hood had not met a wolf before, so she did not know that it was unwise to be too friendly.

"Good day, little girl," said the wolf with a snarly sort of a grin. "What is your name

and where are you going?"
"My name is Little Red
Riding Hood. I am going to
visit my granny, and I am

taking her a cake," replied Little Red Riding Hood.

The wolf was delighted. He thought that with a bit of

planning, he could eat Little Red Riding Hood, her granny AND the cake as well!

"And where does your granny live, little girl?" he asked, trying hard to smile nicely despite his sharp teeth.

Little Red Riding Hood

politely gave the wolf
directions to her granny's
cottage, and went on picking
bluebells. The wolf slipped
away through the trees and
soon found the little house.
He tapped on the door and
said, in as high a voice as he

could manage, "Hello, granny. It is Little Red Riding Hood. I have brought you a cake. Please let me in!"

Granny opened the door, and the wolf bounded in, and gobbled her up! Then he put on her nightcap and shawl and climbed into bed. Soon he heard Little Red Riding Hood coming up the path.

"Hello, granny," said Little Red Riding Hood as she opened the cottage door. "I have brought you a cake and these bluebells."

Then Little Red Riding Hood saw that someone was tucked up in bed. As she got closer she said, "Goodness, Granny! What great big eyes you have!"

"All the better to see you with," replied the wolf.

16

Little Red Riding Hood

Little Red Riding Hood moved a little closer to the bed, and said, "Goodness, Granny! What great big ears you have!"

"All the better to hear you with," growled the wolf.

Then Little Red Riding Hood

came right up next to the bed, and said in surprise, "Goodness, Granny! What great big teeth you have!"

"All the better to eat you with!" snapped the wolf. He leapt out of bed and gobbled Little Red Riding Hood up.

Then he wolfed down the cake in the basket, and then, very full indeed, he fell fast asleep, and snored loudly.

Now by great good luck, a woodcutter was passing by the cottage. He heard the terrible snores and put his

Little Red Riding Hood

head round the door to see who was making the noise.

He was horrified to see the wolf. He took his axe and made a great slit down the wolf's tummy. Out jumped Little Red Riding Hood and Granny.

Granny stitched up the wolf's tummy and told him that he had better mind his manners in future. Then Granny and Little Red Riding Hood went home to Little Red Riding Hood's house for tea.

I am pleased to say Little

Red Riding Hood learnt her lesson, and she never spoke to wolves again.

The End